BOYS

Freaky Snow Dude

...ce Arena and Phil Kettle

illustrated by
Susy Boyer

RISING★STARS

First Published in Great Britain by
RISING STARS UK LTD 2006
22 Grafton Street, London, W1S 4EX

Reprinted 2007, 2008

For more information visit our website at:
www.risingstars-uk.com

British Library Cataloguing in Publication Data

A CIP record for this book is available from the British Library.

ISBN: 978-1-84680-054-2

First published in 2006 by
MACMILLAN EDUCATION AUSTRALIA PTY LTD
15–19 Claremont Street, South Yarra 3141

Visit our website at www.macmillan.com.au or
go directly to www.macmillanlibrary.com.au

Associated companies and representatives throughout the world.

Series created by Felice Arena and Phil Kettle
Project management by Limelight Press Pty Ltd
Cover and text design by Lore Foye
Illustrations by Susy Boyer

Printed in China

UK Editorial by Westcote Computing Editorial Services

Contents

Tom   Joey

CHAPTER 1

Splat!

Best friends Tom and Joey are spending their holidays with Joey's parents at a ski resort. Queuing in their skis, the boys wait for a ski lift to take them to the top of the mountain.

Tom "This is the best holiday I've ever been on in my whole life! Did I say thanks for inviting me?"

Joey "Yes, a million times already."

Tom "I'm really glad that my parents gave me enough money to hire some cool ski gear and take ski lessons with you. Now I'm ... super ski dude."

Joey "I wouldn't say *super*, but you're a heaps better skier than you were five days ago."

Suddenly, two giant snowballs hit the boys—*Splat! Splat!*

Tom "Hey!"
Joey "Who did that?"

Tom and Joey turn to see three older boys on snowboards laughing loudly.

Tom "That stinks! It's those boys again. They've been throwing snowballs at everyone all week."

Joey "And now they got us."

Tom "Let's get them back."

Joey "Are you crazy? Look how big they are."

Tom and Joey ignore the boys, but within moments they are hit again. *Splat! Splat!*

Tom "Ow! That one got me right in the ear."

Joey "Me too. Look! They're heading straight for us."

Tom "We're under attack! What are we going to do?"

Joey "Quick! Jump on!"

Tom and Joey hurriedly hop on to the ski lift only to discover that the older boys have jumped on to the chair behind them. The chase is on.

CHAPTER 2

On the Run

Sitting on the ski lift, Tom and Joey head for the top of the mountain.

Tom "Are they still there?"

Joey "Er, *yes!*—where else are they going to go? They're on a chair, a thousand metres off the ground!"

Tom and Joey look back to see the older boys sneering at them—and still holding some snowballs.

Joey "Right. We're nearly there. When I say go, we have to jump off and ski a hundred miles an hour. If we don't, they'll catch us."

Tom "But I'm still a learner."

Joey "What happened to you being super ski dude?"

Tom "I'm only a super ski dude when I don't have big ski dudes chasing me."

Joey "You'll be alright, just follow me. Ready … go!"

Tom and Joey jump from the ski lift on to the icy slope. Within moments they are flying down the mountain.

Tom and Joey "WHOOOOAAAA!!!!!"

Joey "That's it, Tom! Keep your
knees bent and just look straight
ahead."

Tom "I am! I am!"

The boys swish past other skiers,
darting in and out between them.

Tom (shouting) "There's no way they can catch us now! I wonder if they're behind us?"

Tom looks back.

Joey "Tom, look out!"

Tom turns to see a huge hump
directly in front of him. Before he can
stop, he skis up and over the hump.

Tom "AAAAARRRRGGGHHH!!!!!!!!!"

CHAPTER 3

Crocodile Run

Tom flies through the air and crashes back onto the soft, snowy slope with a thud. Joey swishes up beside him.

Joey "Are you OK?"
Tom "Yes, I think so."

Joey "You were flying! It looked really amazing! Until you landed on your backside and got your skis all tangled up. You sure you're OK?"

Tom "Yes, I think I can still move my legs and arms."

Joey "Good. It doesn't look like you've broken anything. Now, let's get moving! Those snowball attackers will be here any second."

Tom "But I have to put my skis back on."

Joey "We don't have time for that. Quick, follow me!"

Tom and Joey quickly scramble across the slope into the nearby forest just as the older boys swish by.

Joey "Phew! That was close."

Tom "Do you think they saw us?"

Joey "No. We got behind these trees just in time."

Tom "Now what?"

Joey "Well, when they get down to the bottom, they'll see that we're not there and they'll probably wait for us to come down."

Tom "Then they'll bomb us with their snowballs."

Joey "Not if I can help it. I've got a plan."

Joey pulls out a folded map from his pocket.

Tom "What's that?"
Joey "It's a map of all the slopes on the mountain. We're on Crocodile Run at the moment."

Tom "Crocodile Run? What a weird
name for a ski slope. I'd like to see
a crocodile skiing. Maybe it would
bite off the arms of the skiers as it
went along. That'd be *so* cool!"

Joey "Er, are you sure you didn't hit
your head when you fell?"

Tom "Never felt better. Now, what's
the deal with the map?"

Joey "There's another slope not too far from here. We can get there if we walk through the forest. Then we can ski down it and miss those big boys completely."

Tom "Cool. Talk about outsmarting them. Let's go!"

CHAPTER 4

Freaky Snow Dude

Deep in the forest, Joey and Tom slowly march through the snow.

Tom "I think we should go back. We've been walking for ages. I read at the resort that skiers shouldn't leave the slopes—ever! It's dangerous."

Joey "Now you tell me!"

Tom "Well, I didn't know you were going to get us lost, did I?"

Joey "We're not lost."

Tom "No? Then where are we?"

Joey looks around, then back at his map.

Joey "Er, I thought we would see that other slope by now … er … OK … maybe we're a little bit lost."

Tom "Are you serious? Oh no, we're going to die out here. We're going to freeze to death or be eaten by a pack of wolves."

Joey "There aren't any wolves around here. And we can always build an igloo to keep us warm."

Tom "But what about the abomni ... abomni ..."

Joey "The abominable snowman?"

Tom "Yes, that freaky snow dude."

Joey "That's just make believe. It's a made-up story."

Tom "No, it's true. I saw it on TV once. It's like this huge half-man, half-ape creature that lives in the forest. And if it finds us, it will probably pick us up by the feet and have us for dinner."

Suddenly, the sound of a branch snapping echoes through the forest.

Tom "What was that? It's him! The abomni … aboba … aboba … the freaky snow dude!"

Joey "Stop it will you! Now you're scaring me!"

Tom "Look!"

A dark figure appears from the trees.

Tom and Joey "ARRRGGGHHH!!!!!!"

CHAPTER 5

Melting Snowmen

As the dark figure draws closer, Tom
and Joey soon realise that it isn't an
abominable snowman, but a ranger.
The boys sigh, relieved to see him.

Joey "You should have seen your
face. You really thought it was an
abominable snowman."

Tom "No, I didn't."

Joey "Yes, you did. You almost wet
your pants."

Tom "Right, so did you."

The ranger tells the boys that they shouldn't have moved off the slopes. He says that Joey's parents were wondering where they were. Luckily, the ranger had been able to follow Tom and Joey's footprints.

Tom "Told you it was a bad idea."
Joey "No, you didn't."

Tom and Joey march a few steps behind the ranger as he leads them back down to the resort.

Joey "Well, we're saved anyway ... but what would you have done if it really was an abominable snowman? And don't say, run away or scream like a girl."

Tom "Right, as if! No, I would have got my Mum's hairdryers out."

Tom grins at Joey.

Joey "Hairdryers?"

Tom "Yes—one in each hand—and I'd put the settings on really high heat, and blow and melt the freaky snow dude away, until he was just a puddle."

Joey "Yes, I really do think you hit your head when you fell."

The boys make it safely back to the resort and Joey's parents. Their holiday in the snow has come to an end. Joey's parents have packed the car and are ready to leave.

Tom "Hey, look, over there … it's those guys who threw snowballs at us!"

Joey "Yes, and they haven't seen us. Are you thinking what I'm thinking?"

Tom and Joey quickly make some snowballs and throw them at the older boys. *Splat! Splat! Splat!* The three boys turn to chase Tom and Joey but it's too late. They've already jumped into the car and are driving off.

Tom "Hey, Joey, have I told you that
this is the best holiday I've ever
been on in my whole life?"

Tom and Joey laugh. All the older
boys can do is stand and watch the
car drive away. Tom and Joey wave
at them from the back seat.

Tom

Joey

Snow Lingo

abominable snowman A large, hairy creature that lives in the snow. Some people think it's a made-up story and others believe it's real. What do you think?

freaky snow dude An easier way to say abominable snowman—well, at least for Tom it is.

poles The two sticks skiers use to help them keep their balance.

ski lift A whole lot of chairs hanging from a cable. You sit on one, and it takes you to the top of the mountain.

ski run What skiers ski down— sometimes known as a ski slope.

BOYS RULE!
Snow Must-dos

☞ If you want to ski, make sure you have lessons. You especially need to learn how to stop!

☞ When you're out on the ski slopes, watch out for trees. They have a habit of catching you!

☞ Even if you're not a very good skier, you should wear some cool clothes and try to look the part.

☞ If you're skiing down a steep hill and you lose your nerve, just sit on your skis and slide down.

☞ If you don't have skis, go sledging or tobogganing instead—it's just as much fun!

☞ If there's plenty of soft snow around, make some snowballs and have a snowball fight with your friends.

☞ If you're going to throw snowballs at older boys, just be sure you can make a quick getaway.

☞ To get into a "snowy mood", watch some snow-themed films like "Snow Day" or "Snow Dogs", and drink some hot chocolate too!

BOYS RULE!
Snow Instant Info

 Some of the best ski resorts in the world are in the Alps in Europe, Lake Tahoe in America and also in New Zealand. In Britain, one of the best places for skiing is Aviemore in the Cairngorm Mountains in Scotland.

 Skis used to be made of wood, but today, most skis are made out of plastic and polyurethane foam.

 Britain's first (and only!) Olympic ski jumper was Eddie "The Eagle" Edwards. He represented Britain in the 1998 Winter Olympics.

Snowboarding developed from skateboarding. Snowboarding became an Olympic sport in 1998.

 The tallest snowman recorded in the Guinness Book of Records was made in Maine, America. The snowman was 34.63 metres tall!

 Everyone knows that some of the Inuits live in igloos made of ice, but did you know that in Jukkasjarvi, Sweden, there's a hotel made out of ice? It's called the Ice Hotel.

 Snow is crystals of frozen water.

Think Tank

1 What's the one thing you need for a good snowball fight?

2 What's the best way to climb a mountain?

3 What's hot and sweet and best to have after a day of skiing?

4 Do you need ski poles to go snowboarding?

5 Name a British ski jumper who has the initials "EE".

6 How cold does it have to be for it to snow?

7 What's another name for the abominable snowman?

8 Where's the best place to fall?

Answers

1. For a good snowball fight, you need snow, of course! And other people.
2. The best way to climb a mountain is sitting in a ski lift.
3. Hot chocolate is the best thing to have after a day of skiing.
4. No, but you do need a snowboard.
5. Eddie "The Eagle" Edwards is the British ski jumper.
6. It has to be really, really, really cold for it to snow.
7. Another name for the abominable snowman is freaky snow dude.
8. The best place to fall is in really soft snow.

How did you score?

- If you got all 8 answers correct, then go and find yourself a mountain. You were born to have fun in the snow.

- If you got 6 answers correct, then you don't mind a good snowball fight. In fact if it were snowing right now, you wouldn't be reading this—you'd be outside throwing snowballs.

- If you got fewer than 4 answers correct, then you're more of a beach person than a snow dude.

39

Felice →   ← Phil

Hi Guys!

We have heaps of fun reading and want you to, too. We both believe that being a good reader is really important and so cool.

Try out our suggestions to help you have fun as you read.

At school, why don't you use "Freaky Snow Dude" as a play and you and your friends can be the actors. Set the scene for your play. Bring some ski goggles and ski gloves, or perhaps even skis and poles, to school to use as props. Make some fake snowballs out of rolled-up paper.

So ... have you decided who is going to be Tom and who is going to be Joey? Now, with your friends, read and act out our story in front of the class.

We have a lot of fun when we go to schools and read our stories. After we finish the children all clap really loudly. When you've finished your play your classmates will do the same. Just remember to look out the window—there might be a talent scout from a television channel watching you!

Reading at home is really important and a lot of fun as well.

Take our books home and get someone in your family to read them with you. Maybe they can take on a part in the story.

Remember, reading is fun.

So, as the frog in the local pond would say, Read-it!

And remember, Boys Rule!

Felice Arena   *Phil Kettle*

Phil "Do you like snow?"

Felice "I love it. When I was a kid I built this really cool-looking snowman."

Phil "It would be cool … it was made out of snow."

Felice "Ha, ha, very funny. But then this boy came along and kicked it over."

Phil "That's a rotten thing to do. Although, I confess I did that once."

Felice "You did?"

Phil "Yes, I felt really bad for doing it. It was a really cool-looking snowman with a scarf and a red top hat …"

Felice "… with blue stripes?"

Phil "Yes … but how did you …? Oops! Sorry."

What a Laugh!

Q What do snowmen wear on their heads?

A Snow caps!

BOYS RULE!

Gone Fishing	**The Tree House**	**Golf Legends**	**Camping Out**	**Bike Daredevils**
Water Rats	**Skateboard Dudes**	**Tennis Ace**	**Basketball Buddies**	**Secret Agent Heroes**
Wet World	**Rock Star**	**Pirate Attack**	**Olympic Champions**	**Race Car Dreamers**
Hit the Beach	**Rotten School Day**	**Halloween Gotcha!**	**Battle of the Games**	**On the Farm**

BOYS RULE! books are available from most booksellers.
For mail order information please call Rising Stars
on 0871 47 23 010 or visit www.risingstars-uk.com

44